I0533770

Miss Mary is a translation of a French flagellant novel written by Alphonse Momas (1846-1933), a prolific author of erotica (*Miss Mary*, London-Paris [Paris]: Société des Bibliophiles, 1907). Momas used numerous pseudonyms, including, amongst others, Tap-Tap, Pan-Pan, Trix, Fuckwell, and Le Nismois. *Miss Mary* is part of Momas' series, 'Par le fouet et par la verge' — 'By whip and by rod.' It is also the first book in a three volume series set in an elite girls' school in London governed by a harsh disciplinarian, Miss Sticker. The other books in this series are *Miss Grégor* (1907) and *Le Secret de Miss Sticker* (1907).

The English translation of *Miss Mary* bears the publication date 1906 on its title page but, considering that the French original was issued in 1907, this date must be false. *Miss Mary* was most probably published and printed in France and, given the idiosyncratic nature of the translation, was almost certainly translated by someone whose first language was not English.

Chapter headpiece decorations in this Birchgrove Press edition of *Miss Mary* are from another flagellant novel written by Momas, *Fouetteuse*, par Trix (Paris-Bruxelles, 1901). Chapter tail-piece decorations are based on designs in *Fouetteuse*.

The English translation of *Miss Grégor* (London-Paris, Privately printed for the French and English Bibliophiles Society, 1907) is also available from Birchgrove Press.

By whip and by rod

MISS MARY

BY

TAP-TAP

LONDON-PARIS

Privately printed for the French and English

BIBLIOPHILES SOCIETY
1906

BIRCHGROVE PRESS
MMXII

Miss Mary
© The British Library Board P.C.13.ff.24

© Birchgrove Press
2012

All Rights Reserved

ISBN:
978-0-9871953-6-4

http://www.birchgrovepress.com

MISS MARY

BY

TAP-TAP

BY WHIP AND BY ROD

MISS MARY

BY

TAP-TAP

CHAPTER I

It was a big house, in the midst of
gardens, and in front stood a monumental
Terrace; walks were going down slantly on
the three sides, with thickets: such was the
ensemble, one could see at first glance, of
miss Sticker's school for young girls.

There were also high walls running round
the park, adorned with superior branches of
old trees, and such walls helped to the

reputation of first class school this establishment had secured.

One could enter the park by the north lodge of the doorkeeper and the south one of the gardeners, and closed the entrance of the square house to all indiscreet curiosities. When the gates were passed, one was surprised before the richness of the flower-beds, the symmetry of walks full of shade and the whole magnificent organisation of this Eden-School destined to the education of young English misses and also some scions of noble continental families.

All that could recreate the eyes or develop ideal aspirations of the soul were there, in this corner of London's suburbs. And all tourists felt an obsession to visit this foundation of the Sticker dynasty, when in the neighbourhood, they heard the words of praise of all the people. One could visit the school but only during the vacation months when the servants only were in it, and the house seemed deeply asleep.

Curiously, such silent sleep insisted also during the schooling months, for no sound came outside, no cry was ever heard by those even who passed near by.

How did the young misses enjoy themselves, which were their distractions? No
indiscretion ever came out of there.

One could at times however see, through
the gates, the white robes of the pupils and
black dresses of the teachers. There were
fresh and cheeky little faces which had
nevertheless some grave air on them. Never
could one see them running through the
walks, like little girls will do.

Were they happy or not? No one did
know, not even their parents, for they never
complained.

Therefore did the Institute have a
universal repute: friendship began there,
subsisted, when the pupils had left the
school, in the divers phases of life. But,
curiously also, never did any old pupil put
her own children there or advise other
people to put theirs.

They spoke respectfully of the Sticker; but
they never answered praising words they
heard said of them, and seemed to have
completely forgotten the establishment.

At that time, in 1890, miss Sticker was 35
years old, tall, dark-brown, cool, did never
laugh, and looking at pupils with piercing

eyes, brought fright to the very heart of a culprit; she never said an inconsiderate word, playing her part of head school mistress with true British haughtiness.

For her school mistresses as well as for the children she had an implacable severity that constituted her "raison d'être", and to avoid the effects of such severity, good work, and equally wise conduct stimulated all the beings of this house.

In the schools, when she was passing inspection, teachers and pupils alike trembled in their shoes, for fear something had gone wrong and caused a personal or general correction.

Therefore if everything in the ensemble of the house looked charming to heart and soul, it was different when incorporated in it. One had to submit to the inexorable discipline of the head mistress, that is when one came to know the habits and customs of the school.

The number of pupils varied from 60 to 80, and they were divided in 4 classes: the first one for children from 8 to 10; the second from 10 to 12; then from 12 to 15 and the last one from 15 to 18.

Four mistresses and eight under-mistresses conducted the classes, while several solid girls attended to the service, following the orders of a chiefess. Men servants under the special control of miss Sticker were left to the two entrance lodges.

One day in November 1898, a French lady, Mme Loys de Glady entered the head mistress' room introducing her daughter Reine aged 13 she wished to have educated here.

Nice and fair, with long tresses, Reine had blue dreamy eyes, a white and pink complexion, and had more an English type as that of a French girl. Sweet and timid, charming doll, she attracted sympathy at once.

Miss Sticker did not even smile or nod, but said rather hard:

— This is the child, madame, about whom you wrote to me, desiring me to direct her studies and her morality?

—Yes, miss, my daughter, I am certain, will make all efforts to satisfy you and make us forget to her father and myself the reason that obliges us to separate from her.

Miss Sticker rung the bell and said to the

servant that came in:

— Bring miss Reine to Mrs. Clary.

Hearing this Reine wanted to kiss her mother, but miss Sticker prevented her.

— You have wished good-by to your mamma when passing our threshold. It is unnecessary to lose time in superfluous effusions, follow Jenny.

Although troubled, Mme de Glady stiffened and approved the head-mistress and the child went, afraid even to cry.

When the two women were alone, miss Sticker said:

— Be sure, madame, that your daughter will receive here all cares her health necessitates. You'll be proud of her as regards instruction and education, and later on she won't give you any cause for sorrow.

The mother cried and answered:

— I know, miss, and it's the reason that made us take her away from France and bring her to you. Reine is a capital child, but of a very feeble character that was the cause of her shocking fault.

— You surprised her?

— With her lady cousin, in a shameful position.

— And the lady cousin?...

— Is older than our child. She is twenty and — I had taken her by charity: but we were to avoid such a scandal to hurt Reine in her future.

— You did your duty. We'll efface the shame of this poor soul.

— May god inspire you!

Miss Sticker got up, making Mme de Glady understand that the conversation was finished.

CHAPTER II

The pupils of third and fourth class only slept in private rooms, therefore Reine entering the third one was given a separate room.

It was really a little cell, furnished with a bed, a cupboard, two chairs and a washstand.

Mrs. Clary to whom Jenny brought her, was a fair woman of thirty, neither handsome nor ugly, who had charge of that class but also the general survey of the school. She did not impose like miss Sticker, but was also not sympathetic. She interrogated Reine, about her knowledge and could not help pulling a face.

— You'll have to work hard, my child, because your companions are far more advanced.

If the room was simply furnished, luxury was everywhere noticeable in the corridors, in the school-rooms and assembly rooms, where everything was in harmony to inspire the taste of the handsome to the pupils.

One thing especially called Reine's attention, when she entered the school-room; on the walls was everywhere written in big letters:

"By whip and by rod!"

In vain did she look at her companions, none of them looked up from their books to wish her welcome by a nod only. There was a dead silence: for the implacable hand of the head mistress broke down all these young minds.

The under-mistress, a plump little woman of somewhat twenty, miss Gregor, approached and sat down by her side, which was easy, as every desk was separated.

She gave her in a low tone rules of the house: getting up with day break, bed-time at nine; day divided by studies, recreations, walks in the park, useful conversations.

Absolute prohibition to all pupils to get friendly together, or to speak about any subject other than their lessons or advice given to them.

They could write once a month to their parents by an open letter submitted to the head-mistress.

At once, with her feeble character, the child felt an instinctive fright. She closed her eyes, and pulled her arms forward, as searching for help.

— What's the matter, asked miss Gregor?

— Nothing, miss, nothing.

From that moment she understood she'd have to dissimulate her least impressions. A French girl among such little English misses, she would know how to work and deliver herself from the slavery she presented.

She asked from miss Gregor the explanation of the wording of the walls:

"By whip and by rod."

This the under-mistress did giver her — miss Sticker's excellent method of education rested on moral domination by fear of corporal punishment. One did not wish to punish, but at the least fault, a suit of graduated correction tamed the most rebel natures.

— I hope, miss Reine, we shall only seldom have to give them to your little person.

— I hope I shall never have them.

— Your answer shows pride, and you were not a new one, this would cause your first correction. Think always before answering.

Reine shook her head and promised herself to show them that they would not act with a French girl as with English ones.

School-life began, and by her application, and sweet character she showed off, Reine had good notes. She conformed herself to all rules, evaded all trifling faults, so not to be punished, and that terror showed that miss Sticker's system had some good in it.

In her young heart, Reine had a notion that the human body is sacred and no hand must touch it with violence, under any pretext.

With all good intentions, when one is 13 years old, there are times where a fault can be committed.

Waking up one morning, more gay than usual, she hummed some Paris song, forgetting one was not permitted to sing.

Stupor of miss Sticker and all her staff! How shocking! To sing, when silence was to be the rule, not even in recreations, a French girl alone could commit such a crime!

Miss Gregor half-dressed called in her room like a bomb, exclaiming:

— Are you mad, miss Reine? You sing!

— Pardon me, miss, I felt happy!

— You felt happy! Well, you'll cry to-night.

You must never feel happy, it is an insult to the poverty of poor devils.

A voice spoke behind miss Gregor:

— Miss Gregor, how dare you admonish a pupil in such neglected and indecent state?

The teacher is as guilty as the pupil and will also be punished.

— Oh, miss Sticker!

— Leave at once and go to finish dressing! Miss Reine, you'll not assist to class this morning: Jenny will bring you to the meditation room.

— I did not know I was doing wrong.

— You'll remember another time.

Not a word more was exchanged, and miss Sticker went away cool and dignified.

Coming down with her companions, Reine noticed content in their looks. It hurt her and she swore that she would have revenge. But she dissimulated again, thinking that for such a trifle she could not possibly be corporally punished.

At the door of the study, Jenny was awaiting to bring her to the meditation room, a large square room with a few chairs and benches and every where the wording:

"By whip and by rod!"

No carpet, no curtains, but at the windows panes of glass whose polish and been taken off to intercept the light.

Two hours long Reine stayed there solitary, seeing only this superficial furniture and the threat on the walls that made her tremble.

These words whip and rod were damning before here eyes, filling her with fear and temper, unknowing what was going to happen.

After the two hours miss Sticker came in with miss Gregor, and turning her face to Reine, while she sat down herself on a chair, she inquired if the girl had meditated.

— About what, madame?

— Your fault.

— Yes, I've been wrong, but in France one sings about any thing.

— Not at school, and if it was so, it is wrong; you are under my care, and I'll give you back to your parents an accomplished young lady. However taking to account what you have been up to now in one school, your punishment will be light. We hope you'll not oblige us to have recourse to force, that would aggravate your case, and you'll be only punished in my presence. Please pull up your dress.

— Pull up my dress?

— Passive obedience and no observation, miss, pull up your dress.

— What for?

— Pull them up on your arms to be flogged as you deserve it, but only with the hand. This would be transformed in flagellation with the whip or rod, if you keep on answering.

— To flog me! I forbid you. I've never been flogged when I was little, and won't be now that I'm a big girl!

— A big culprit miss! intervened miss Gregor. Submit gently. I also have observed the whip, to have entered your room half-dressed. I'll have to suffer it before you with resignation. Why should you revolt?

— I won't show you...

— Your bottom-cheeks? Were you so proud when you were hiding with you lady-cousin?

— Miss Sticker?

— Will you pull up your dress or shall I have to call the servants to tie you down, undress you and fustigate you with the rod and that before all the assembled pupils.

— No, no, I'll obey.

Reine pulled up her dress, and put it on her arms. Miss Gregor advanced, opened both sides of the drawers, pulled up the chemise and the little moon appeared, round and white, all timid, with its fine upright slit in the middle. With a brutal movement, miss Sticker put the child on her knees, right across, the bottom well naked under her eyes, and she measured it with the hand: she held it so, with a troubled look in her eyes, got up the right hand and hit with all her might. Reine jumped up and wanted to kick: one of miss Sticker's arms leant on her back to keep her there and the flogging multiplied resounding and marking the flesh with red marks, bringing trepidations in the legs, twisting the calves already nice and round.

The more Reine struggled, and the more the hand became hard and pitiless, hitting hard until, suddenly, the resistance ceased and the child stopped inert, passive: slight spasms moved the top of the cheeks; a sardonic smile stopped on miss Sticker's lips, she whipped no more, helped Reine up, whose face was purple and eyes looked mad.

— Your punishment is over, said miss Sticker; try not to be at fault again, for it would bring a severe punishment. No one escapes punishment in this house. Your under-mistress has been at fault, so that you, her pupil, you'll whip her. Miss Gregor, put yourself on the bench.

In the middle of the piece was a stuffed bench, higher up at one extremity. Without hesitation, miss Gregor put herself on it, upon her belly, and miss Sticker taking hold of a short handled whip with three leather bands, very hard, gave it to Reine and said:

— Hit miss Gregor's bottom with this, as hard as you ever can.

— Oh, miss?

— Stop that nonsense and protest! Do you wish to feel it also? No? Well, once and for all, do submit without a word! Go, miss Gregor, pull up your dress and show your moon.

The under-mistress obeyed and showed a pair of plump cheeks exciting with their graceful curve and whiteness, that came out on her wide and powerful thighs, showing in the slit, the vulva, such appetising fruit, that seemed to smile to the child which circumstances were transforming in an executioner.

Was the view of such feminine sexualities opened before the looks of the one who had been the lustful toy of an older cousin and had learnt the art of voluptuous caresses, awakening in her some passed remembrance, but she became white, and turned on herself, ready to kneel down to bring her lips on such riches, which she was ordered to hit!

Miss Sticker's voice was heard:

— Will you hit, miss Reine, or is your perverted soul caressing some filthy images?

A ferocious resolution went in the child's mind: she pulled the whip up and brought it down with surprising energy, hitting so hard that the leather got right in the flesh, livid at first, then purple, leaving all the marks, even bleeding on certain places. Miss Gregor howled, then a second, third, fourth blow that made her jump up like a carp in water, kick up her bottom, hurt the thighs in hard movement on the sides of the bench, although she did not try to get away.

On the contrary she tried to keep her dress up, when it was coming down, through her movements, on her martyrised bottom. She did not cry but sighed, while the blows were coming harder down.

Reine's arms were getting fatigued now, an unknown torpor took possession of her and a mist covered her look, before the blood that began to run down.

— Enough! said miss Sticker. Now take in that cupboard some water, a sponge and a basin. Go and wash miss Gregor's wounds: the corrections are over. Remember, miss Reine, that these organs have not been created to induce us to the sin of lust, but to help us to expiate our faults and make us better.

As a drunken woman, Reine obeyed at

once. Miss Gregor remained inert, down on the bench, her dress still up, with the bottom naked. Slowly the child washed the blood that ran down, but contemplating the under-mistress' sexuality, she noticed with surprise that the vulva was swollen and secreting a white kind of wet. She washed it, as she had done for the blood.

Miss Gregor could not help showing a shiver under the care taken by Reine.

— All right, said miss Sticker at last. Now back to your class and try not to sin any more.

— Miss Gregor is still bleeding!

— That's my business. Go.

Reine went, her mind all over trouble, but thinking herself lucky to have had that correction only.

At school no one said any thing and she resumed her work.

The door closed on Reine, miss Sticker said to miss Gregor:

— You are impure, and you have nearly awakened the French girl's imagination. Your concupiscency has been stronger than the suffering of the torture, and luxury showed itself in your thighs. You'll be on bread and water for three days.

— Is it my fault?

— Get up, and if the whip produces such effect on you, I'll correct you with the red hot irons.

But, miss Gregor got up, went on her knees and kissing her hand, exclaimed:

— Do not be cruel, miss, you know well that here we all only wish to satisfy you and to help you in your noble mission.

— Go and heal your wounds, miss Gregor, and be always strict with your pupils: this house must remain a model house of education, by its severity and its silence.

CHAPTER III

Reine went to work again so well that there was no reason to punish her. But her correction and that of miss Gregor had left in her mind a sort of anguish that weighed heavy on her.

She witnessed twice corporal punishments given to big girls and they gave her a terror that confirmed the wish she already had to promptly finish her schooling.

One was a fair young lady, miss Mary Antterson, a fine English type of girl 17 years old who uttered insulting words addressed to an under-mistress; the report made to miss Sticker brought on a general punishment for all the big girls and the great flagellation with exposure for the culprit.

One evening, after the class was over, the girls grouped by divisions, were brought to a round subterranean room, where they took seat on pews set around a central pillar and a bed covered with a blue velvet cloth.

The under-mistresses were watching that silence would be kept.

Miss Sticker and the four school mistresses appeared and sat down on arm chairs facing the pillar. Then the culprit, miss Mary, entered dressed up in her white feast day's robe, arms tied up and held by the two servants.

Her look anxious and sad was nice and gracious, while her waist showed a young lady that was still a girl.

Whatever passed through her mind to insult an under-mistress and deserve this correction?

The punishment began by a severe talk from the school mistress who spoke with indignation of a girl's rebellion against the persons who devoted themselves to her education. She ended by expressing her satisfaction for the severity that was to meet such action.

After this, on a sign from miss Sticker, the girl was untied and ordered to undress entirely.

— Never, answered miss Mary!

— Undress her, was miss Sticker's order to the servants.

A short struggle ensued: the girl bit and scratched, but the servants were strong and exasperated with resistance; one paralysed her moves while the other one undid all her dress, although she tried to kick.

Many girls were pitying their companions but none offered to go to deliver her, because miss Sticker's discipline had tamed the minds, through years of schooling.

At last, miss Mary was now naked.

— Tie her to the pillar, arms and legs, shouted miss Sticker.

They had no difficulty, for the girl was passive and inert now, and as she was facing miss Sticker, this one came to her and said:

— This rotten flesh intends to master my house by insults and beating! Now you, mistresses and pupils, look at this body made of dirt and shame, do you think it is to inspire pride and silliness? I only see here an ugly flesh that must be corrected.

Miss, you'll be punished by the whip and by the rod, but before that all the pupils, young and old, will defile before you and see what little you are.

Miss Mary cried and did not answer. According to instruction they all passed by her, laughing at the pussy that showed itself provocating already above the nest it shaded, chaffing on order and, as human nature is as coward as ever, even in such little hearts of aristocracy, the girls pleased themselves by insults to the culprit.

After that miss Mary's position was changed, and her back turned to the audience. With a whip, one of the servants, after twisting the lanyard through space sent a terrible blow on the girl's legs.

Mary howled but in vain! How the whip was going, going, turning, whistling and cutting the flesh of thighs, cheeks and back! While all the time the tortured one howled, crying for mercy!

Some of the girls wanted to ask for pity too, but with one severe look from the mistresses everything went right in order again.

Then the whip was at work, but its blows

were not like the blows applied from near, and which tore up and made bleed. But miss Sticker did not want to torture, she only wanted to touch the imagination and the moral, by beating the body. That was her method.

Miss Mary's bottom cheeks must have made curious and amusing contortions, according to the smile on mistresses' and pupils' lips.

The cheeks moved convulsively, opening and closing as if they wanted to catch hold of the lanyard. But at a last blow, the girl howled: "I am dead!"

All the cruel little girls burst out laughing but miss Sticker got up in a temper and stopped such hilarity:

— Shocking! said she. Fancy, taking pleasure at seeing the punishment of a companion! So you all want to go thro' it?

Coming near the girl, miss Sticker, felt her cheeks and back:

— When one is so tender, one must be more careful of what one says. Your skin of a bitch is hardly marked! and we are only beginning.

— Pity!

— Undo her and put her on the bed!

In no time her order was executed.

— Lay her down, and tie her up so that she won't be able to move.

— Pity!

— So do not annoy me with your silly interruptions, replied miss Sticker, if you do not wish all your companions to come and beat you one after the other.

On the bed, miss Mary turned and twisted trying not to be tied up. But the two servants managed her: one sat on her back, while the other tied the cords at the feet, and the bottom being up a trifle received a good beating while the arms were being tied up.

The bottom was high up now; and the two servants placing themselves each on one side of the bed, rod in hand, on a sign from miss Sticker, the blows came down, cutting upon the dear young bottom, that even now tried to evade such blows. One could only hear the flesh crackling and the howling of the young lady.

Now, the blood was coming and some of the pupils were crying.

The under-mistress, cause of the punishment, now got up:

— Enough miss Sticker, the punishment will serve!

— Miss Antterson is a bad pupil, a coquette who deserves to be punished. But as you implore, I pardon. I wanted this harpy to stay in bed for a fortnight, with her cheeks in pieces.

Miss Mary cried less now.

— Let each division, continued miss Sticker, pass by this great culprit and see what the fault is worth.

They all passed around the bed where miss Mary was still laying and tied up, and then could all see her bleeding bottom, while the servants stood up on each side, rod in hand. Such a sight was to be engraved in all hearts, for every one knew a similar torture was awaiting them for a similar offense. They trembled more than being excited by the contemplation of their companion's sexuality.

Reine, however, as troubled as the others, did feel a curiosity: she had tasted the cup of lust, had almost vibrated, when she had seen the secret lips of miss Gregor, and she felt a pain when seeing such lovely flesh maculated by blood, and noticing the nervous jerks which at times showed between the fat of the thighs, the juvenile vulva, full of trouble in its virginity.

Long she remembered such sight of gentle nakedness spoilt by blood, but offering itself as an object of pleasure.

And lust was now born in her soul, annihilating the thought of the danger that may result of it.

Days and weeks passed and the work of desire slowly operated its work; miss Mary was healed of her wounds, and had taken her place back amongst the big girls.

No opportunity presented itself to bring the French girl in contact with the English teacher. And besides, of what use would it be, it was now about vacation time, and that left no hope in Reine's heart.

Let us note that this child, a cousin with very active senses debauched, struggled energetically against temptations: she knew the importance of the "œuvre de chair".

She was well aware how to apply the mouth on the place on heat, on the shivering clitoris, so as to produce ecstasy: her cousin had initiated, guided her in her innocence, teaching her where to put the sides of the face upon her thighs, so as to better give the tongue licks and to better tickle in the sexualities; her cousin taught her the "feuilles de rose", where the bottom-cheeks were turning all-over under the coeting of the kisses.

And, knowing all that, seeing miss Mary from afar, now and then, she could hardly resist to confess what she knew and to beg her on her knees to allow her to make her come, as she had made her cousin come before.

She could not talk to her, as miss Mary belonged to the division of the big girls. She reasoned so as not to look at her with too much fixity, but, by a phenomenon of magnetism, miss Mary looked at her and smiled each time they were close by, either when divisions were going to meals or walking in the park.

When vacation time arrived, Reine felt a great trouble, when she knew that miss Mary having deserved one of the gravest punishments in the school, would not be going to pass the holidays with her people.

With four other pupils, Reine also was to stay: as distraction, miss Sticker would receive them in a small property she had in Scotland, so that under her direction and that of miss Gregor, they would profit of the mountain air.

Reine who was just about 14 then, was consoled of her people's severity after that.

"By whip and by rod", the terrible motto danced all night before her eyes, when she thought of a possible intimacy between this charming young woman and herself. She met her incidentally coming out of the economat, and miss Mary gave her a look, that seemed to want to read through her heart. Reine became so red that miss Mary asked her if she was ill?

— No, I have had such pleasure.

— Ah, said miss Mary, smiling and running away, so as not to be seen talking to a third class pupil. Reine felt now a tickling coming all over her, she never had any thing like it with her cousin! No doubt, she must be amorous of miss Mary, mad in love with her.

All the pupils had left now, and there was semi-liberty at school. Miss Sticker went first to Scotland, leaving the house to the care of miss Gregor and a servant. And this mistress did not annoy anybody, as long as one talked sense and there was no noise.

Miss Mary did not seem to take any notice of such privilege and spent her time with one of the four girls left behind, one of her class, who was very ugly indeed.

Reine felt very hard such indifference on her part, and was in despair having no chance of talking to miss Mary, when they both one day met on the terrace. Reine was looking in a dreamy sort of manner.

— What's the matter, Reine, said miss Mary, dreaming about your country?

— No. About something else!

— What then?

— You, Mary.

— About me?

Miss Mary blushed: had the fruit been already bitten? She hesitated, ready to run away.

— Yes, about you, Mary. I should love to be your friend.

— Pity you are not amongst the big girls! I have the same desire as you to be friends. But the discipline of the school forbids it.

— Even when travelling?

— Then it is difficult. Now, listen, miss

Gregor writes long letters every afternoon and forgets us then. Meet me then in the music-room, there is no survey there.

— What? No survey?

The ground trembled under Reine's feet: her passion was most ardent. Miss Mary ran away!

CHAPTER IV

The music room was a vast gallery with several pianos, harpes, mandolines, an organ and where it was very easy to get isolated. Miss Mary was there, looking at some musical books.

— Here I am, Mary, said Reine.

— Nice of you to have thought of our little rendez-vous! You interest me, but you amuse me also, because you make me feel funny when you look at me.

— Why?

— You seem to be a little lover.

— Oh yes, I do love you!

— Ah, said miss Mary, putting down her

book.

— Yes, continued Reine, I'm a little lover who knows how to love and to give pleasure.

Miss Mary became pale and murmured:

— Who taught you, Reine?

— A cousin of mine, who knew things. And you, you know it too?

— I guess it. So you will love me and give me that pleasure you know of?

— Yes! I'll love you and caress you where you have been wounded by spite.

— Quiet, Reine: walls can hear. But how will you love me so, we shall never be alone?

— So you would let me?

— Loved by you, oh yes! It seems to me I should feel such beatitude.

— Yes, I'll give you such caresses everywhere, on what is hidden under the dress.

— Quiet, quiet, we'll never be able to do it!

— Tell me where your room is. I'll brave any thing to go there.

— They'd skin us alive, my dear, if we were found out.

— I want to love and caress and suck you,

and shall risk any thing. Are you afraid?

— Yes, but I want your caresses where you say. I remember the rod! But I am as mad as you: I can't resist the desire you excite in me. Now look here, there is a place: the infirmary. To-night I'll sleep there, saying I have head-ache. Find some excuse, some illness at night, and they'll send you there too and we'll meet.

— Right!

— Now, let us part, so that nobody will notice our absence.

— Let me kiss you before.

— No I am afraid, not here, go away!

She had gone back behind a grand piano, not noticing that she gave Reine every chance, as no one could see them there.

Reine had followed her in this hiding place, went on her knees and dipped her head under miss Mary's dress. The last named pulled them up herself, saying:

— We are mad, but give me a caress quick, so that I shall know!

The drawers, which were closed, being in the way, she undid it in haste, letting it fall on her legs, for she wanted to be gamahushed as much as the other wanted to gamahush her.

— Make haste!

Reine saw again the flesh she had been so often dreaming of! She was mad with joy for she was to direct the volupty, rule the senses of Mary, as she knew of her inexperience.

Mary was now standing firmly on her calves approaching the thighs, the cunt from the lips.

Triumph of flesh sympathising with flesh! A magnetic current was between Reine's face and Mary's secret parts. Reine kissed and licked the cunt, kissing also the curve of the thighs and even the hips, while Mary now was bending on her legs and, showing the clitoris with the finger, she murmured:

— A kiss, a lick there also.

The "minettes" became burning: both had lost all reason. Reine, at the summum of her lustful joy was the first to come back to prudence. After a last, long caress, she put Mary's drawers in place:

— You are my beloved, Mary.

— Yes, and you are my little lover.

She was sorry of the stopping of the caresses.

— Be reasonable, Reine continued, and to-night I'll promise you ecstasy.

Mary took her by the waist, and begged for a kiss on the mouth.

— That is love too, said she, a young cousin of mine always kissed me there.

By whip and by rod! Never mind! One would go through fire when the desire of flesh pushed one being towards another! Never mind what people say. Against inverted loves: a woman loves a woman, a girl loves a girl, and a man loves a man. The flesh gets excited, and makes criminals, because one intends to tame it. But it makes heroes also.

That child felt capable of any thing to go and join her beloved at her nocturnal rendez-vous.

The infirmary, in this so well combined school, was the only neglected place for survey, as miss Sticker thought that illness annihilated the mind. It contained 6 beds, and although under supervision of a nurse, no one ever came to disturb the girls in their sleep.

Mary did not meet any difficulty to go there early in the evening. Reine also found easy access to it, complaining of a splitting head-ache.

About ten o'clock, when the nurse had gone, they were alone at last. Mary waited, as is usual for the beloved, and her lover Reine did not make her wait too long. They occupied beds rather far from one another, but a heavy curtain hiding the medicine cupboard allowed them to get in to bed easy again in case of surprise.

Reine crossed the room, going to Mary, and found her, the elbow on the pillow, waiting.

— Dear little lover!

Before the bed, Reine bent down and both kissed on the mouth, but such kisses are not half as inspiring as the others on the genital parts. Reine pulled back the sheets, pulled up the chemise, put down her head between the thighs, found out the clitoris, and tickled it quickly with the tongue, with all the science she had learnt in France.

— Ah! ah! ah! sighed Mary, what joy! I love you, go, go, again, for ever! I lose my head!

Reine had struggled so long against her desire, that before her friend's voluptuous tenderness and such flesh that was really hers, her puberty spoke. She nearly cried all her passionate lust:

— Ah, my beloved, Mary, Mary, I am dying with joy.

She stayed motionless on Mary's belly, and the other caressing her cheeks said:

— Have a rest, darling.

Reine did not move. Mary waited a moment, then sat down, and feeling then the hot and wet caress of her mouth on her navel, she made her get up on the bed and received her in her arms. Their two bodies were embraced, belly to belly, kissing, kicking the back, getting so excited that they were all wet, coming together:

— Oh, we piss with happiness and joy, we are little dirty girls, my Reine.

— No, we don't piss, we are coming. I'll draw up your stuff.

— Yes, draw it; afterwards you'll lick the other side, so that I shall know the difference.

— I'll lick you any where.

As Reine was going down the bed again, Mary turned her bottom towards her face and said:

— Lick it, to efface the blows.

— Oh the dear darling, isn't it a splendid one!

Reine adored to make any kind of caress. She was so prodigal of "feuilles de rose", that Mary moved about, murmuring:

— Oh it's good, it's better. Keep on, lick deeply, lick the innerest!

She opened the slit with both hands, so that her little friend could put the tongue further still. The cheeks were moving about even more than under the whip. However, after a short coming, Mary stopped the caresses, saying:

— Enough, it would kill you. Let us sleep both in our bed, so as not to be surprised.

— I could have continued. Who knows when we'll be able to do it again?

— Not every day, it would be dangerous.

Reine left her with regret, but Mary was so tired!...

Next morning the governess noticed nothing, and both pretended to be indifferent to one another. So they were also all day long, and at last Reine grew wild, as she had wished a rendez-vous for the evening.

She was very surprised to see miss Gregor stop her, as she was going to enter her room.

— Miss Reine, if I seem not to see, all the same I know many things. You have committed a great fault. Come with me.

Reine was astounded! Did miss Gregor guess her love for Mary?

She entered miss Gregor's room, which was comfortably furnished.

Miss Gregor sat down on an armchair and said:

— According to the satisfaction you'll give me, I shall know if I must address a report to miss Sticker or not. Kneel down and confess.

— Confess?

— Kneel down there. I have a right to chastise you personally. There's the whip you used with me. You remember?

— Yes, miss.

— You were not ill to-night.

— Yes I was.

The whip went up.

— Don't whip, cried Reine.

— Were you ill?

— Yes.

— Undress!

— Oh, miss!

— Obey!

— Don't hit me, for mercy! I know I hit you but it was no fault of mine.

— You remember what you saw?

Reine was no fool. Miss Gregor's ways did seem strange to her, for every time she wanted to place herself aside, the teacher brought her back between her legs.

— I remember, miss, you were so lovely.

— You looked then?

She took Reine's hand and pressed it very suggestively between her thighs.

— I want your caresses, you understand me? You were silly to run after miss Mary, and you would have understood what I wanted. You'll caress me?

— Yes, miss. I know you'll come with what I'll do. But you'll close your eyes. I love miss Mary, but she was sulky to-day. I was very sorry.

— Be nice with me, I'll be the same with you but I don't like you running after miss Mary. It can be known and I don't want to be compromised.

— I won't say any thing, even if they beat me to death or skin me alive.

Miss Gregor smiled and added:

— With that doll of Mary, follow my

advice: Be firm and even hit her, it'll be the only way to secure her. But, enough said. Now, show me your talent, quick go hereunder and violate me.

Refined, miss Gregor wanted to have the idea of being seeked for by young Reine, and she did not do anything to bring the girl under her dress. Reine understood, and sneaked between her legs, and noticing the absence of drawers she saw with emotion the powerful thighs, the well-furnished pussy, the swollen vulva, and pulling the dress high up she caressed the navel with her tongue, brought the lips down to the pussy, found the clitoris, sucked it, put her mouth on the cunt and gave her a few minettes.

These woman's thighs abandoned to her caresses woke up her sensuality: miss Gregor's sexuality revealed itself by her perfume of woman on heat, and the girl pumped up that heat which she was surprised to find a volupty to aspire, to kiss and lick the best she could.

She wanted now to uplift the teacher's legs, so as to put her tongue everywhere.

— Bring a chair, said miss Gregor, I'll put

my feet on the back and you'll have before your eyes all what you want to caress. You are a lovely "gougnotte".

Reine took the advice at once: the teacher put her legs well up in the air, half laying down on the edge of the arm-chair, the petticoats right up on the breast, showing thus the wide opening of the cunt between the legs, and the bottom too up to the back, with two superb cheeks, halved by the fascinating slit.

Reine took place in the midst of all that flesh and luxurious under-clothing.

— Oh, said she, it's even nicer as when I hit it.

— You like that so?

— Oh yes.

— Lick me, and put your face to it.

— Yes, oh yes!

— You are so hot, are you coming?

— I am all wet.

— Come and show me, darling.

— No, after I'll have caressed you.

— Right! Do it well, I shall soon come and we'll pass to other pleasures. Oh! you know how to manoeuvre the finger also in the bottom-hole?

— No, it's only inspiration!

She was doing her "minettes" and did not think then about her beloved Mary. The formed woman acted on her temperament and before such beautiful treasures, she was losing breath! The swollen vulva was trembling and stupefied Reine. The clitoris pointed out, the vagina uncovered, while the cheeks were moving about, inviting to all temerities. And then the bottom-hole closing as soon as she put her finger in... there was enough to satisfy her lust!

She was remembering the whipping she had given to the cheeks that pleased her so now: she saw the blood coming to the flesh... and there she heard the oppressed breath of miss Gregor, showing she took more pleasure than pain at such flagellation.

The tongue was working, active and unfatigued; and the teacher's volupty could be noticed by the spasms of her belly. She knocked with her thighs on Reine's face in quicker and quicker repetition. A last jerk, more accentuated, wetted her face with the coming spunk, and Reine swallowed it with avidity.

Miss Gregor's hands were caressing her

head, pressing it on her cunt and sending it back: and for the first time of her life, Reine was tossing herself off.

The teacher understood it, took her in her arms and with her legs across her own knees, made her lean back, put her hand under her dress and tickled with joy that young clitoris.

— Ah, exclaimed Reine, I'm coming in your hand!

— Come, darling, I had all I expected from your caresses: my joy is great to give you pleasure too.

A shiver moved the whole body of the child, who pressing against the teacher, looked in her eyes and both kissed on the lips.

They looked tenderly at each other, and the teacher had no shame to have debauched her pupil, for she knew the story of the cousin, and the story with Mary. She wanted now to accaparate Reine for herself, but moved by some strange thought, she put her down, and trying to be severe:

— We made a fault together, Reine. If miss Sticker knew of it, she would punish us cruelly. She is not here, it is right that we should punish ourselves. Undress yourself, I'll whip you and you'll whip me afterwards.

— You wish it?

— Certainly, dear, and I hope you'll submit without protest. She did not look spiteful. Reine presented that such punishment was to be an initiation: she sent her a kiss through the fingers, pulled up her dress most cheekily, when such act was so monstrous to her before. Her bottom, not yet characterised by opulent shapes, appeared seductive, with its little apples, already appetizing by the fulguration of a flesh ready to vibrate under lascivious desires.

Miss Gregor kneeled down, caressed it with the hand, getting knowledge of its fullness, and let the thumb go all along the slit, while she murmured:

— I'll flog you with the hand first, I don't want to hurt you. I want you to love to be whipped so that you'll understand the joy it procures to the one who receives it and the one who gives it.

— Yes, miss. Flog me first, then the whip, it seems to me that if it makes the blood run, I'll feel a supreme felicity!

— Ah, darling, why do you go on loving

that silly miss Mary?

— I am not thinking about her now, and then, it isn't the same as with you!

— You prefer her?

— No it is not what I wish to say! With miss Mary, I want something I ignore as yet, but with you, miss Gregor... well you'll be cross!

— Speak out, dear.

— All your flesh dominates me... I feel you all what dirty things are... and that you wish to teach them to me, so that I should be your little gougnotte... very dirty... by making you come... and coming also.

— Lovely gougnotte!

— Your own!

Miss Gregor got up and gave a first little flogging. Reine cried out:

— Harder, so that your hand should burn my bottom!

— You call it "cul" in France.

— Oh, miss, we say "derrière".

— Yes, and "cul"; say my "cul" when we are together.

— Right you are.

The teacher flogged with more roughness and Reine's bottom became red: she trembled on her legs, as the blows were becoming harder. She felt an afflux of blood that surprised her, and the hand hitting with more vigour, she approached, as if calling for blows.

— Ah, miss, give me the whip, but be all naked to give it to me.

— Oh, you, pearl of France, you ask for it yourself? My hand already gives you pleasure in flogging you.

— My head is swimming, the blood pricks me every where, I want to lick you again, to suck you. Let me do it, miss, so much that you'll come very quickly.

— No, you'll whip me before I undress, and then I'll give it to you in turn. I want to know how far goes your intelligence. I'll lay down on my bed and will judge by the way you'll uncover me... what?

— Your "derrière".

— No.

— Your "cul".

— And what.

— Your thighs.

— No, the hole, the "trou"?

— Your "trou du cul".

— There, a kiss on my lips, now, that I

have well kissed your dear "cul"; it will put me right, and you'll see that I am as good as all the Mary Anttersons of the world.

Miss Gregor was enthusiastic about that little French Girl who understood so well what she wanted. She eated almost her bottom cheeks, and Reine began to think that to receive caresses had also great charm.

The teacher's tongue joined the lips and sometimes glided between the thighs, while Reine awaited with more and more emotion what the teacher would do to her, intending to greatly repay her afterwards. Now she felt her undoing her dress and bodice, taking them off and ordering her to take off her chemise, an order she obeyed at once and there she was naked before miss Gregor still on her knees behind her bottom. Oh! what was she doing? Her tongue was pointing through her cheeks and was getting into her slit, pricking her little bottom-hole and then getting up the slit right above the back, coming down to get in the slit again, and it was a debauche of licking, sucking, feuilles de rose, etc., which Reine had given to others but was having for the first time herself.

The teacher stopped the fever that excited

her to bring the trouble of joy in her young pupil, got up, ran to her bed and laid down, turning her back. Without a word, and not embarrassed to be naked, Reine followed her, pulled up her dress, uncovering first the calves, the thighs, the cheeks strong and predominating, the beginning of the slit well accentuated down the back, the waist developing the robust hips. Miss Gregor put a finger about the middle of the slit of her bottom and asked:

— What is there? the "trou" of what?

— Of your "cul"; shall I whip it?

— With the tongue first.

— How delicious!

She threw herself with avidity upon this complacent back, touched it with both hands, felt it all over with gourmand tongue, and then the teacher stopped her at last.

She ordered:

— Quick, the whip, make me bleed, I deserve it for my odious conduct.

Reine had the whip in hand, and contemplated the two cheeks which hoped for a correction: she shivered in her young body about all that was lascivious in the act she was asked to do: she certainly ignored nothing of her cousin's sexualities, but the vision was always troubled by the fear of her parents, and about miss Mary's sexualities, the fire of her passion covered them like of a mist!

Miss Gregor presented what was going on in her heart, and gave seductive movements to her flesh, which finished hypnotising the girl: she turned the cheeks, rolled over, so as to show the slit in all sorts of positions, and at last, putting her hand to her bottom, said:

— Come on, hit now!

Reine hit about ten blows so hard that the teacher rolled herself up in a ball, head in hands, bottom right up, the thighs well open, showing the vulva.

At such view, Reine stopped the flagellation, threw her hand forward and pressed the vulva in her little fingers. Miss Gregor suddenly wetted, and the girl wished to pass her head beneath to the lick the wet, but miss stopped her:

— No, no, hit me still, it would not come out enough.

The arm resumed its work; the blows became harder and harder, and the cheeks were full of red marks, blood even was coming up: the chastised one did not complain but was moving about under the erotic passion, and did not cease saying:

— Again, again, still, you spare me, I'll tear up your "cul", if you don't hit harder.

Reine's arm was going at full force, but a mist came before her eyes: she saw miss Gregor laying on her belly, moving her bust and legs, while the slit, in a vertiginous movement seemed to open and close, and now the teacher murmured:

— Your tongue, I'm melting! Quick your kisses!

The thighs opened, and a slight way offering itself under the belly, Reine glided in promptly and sucked the clitoris, while miss Gregor's belly was hitting her forehead, and her vagina was pissing in her mouth all its juice of love!

Never had she been at such a feast; she was like drowned between the teacher's thighs, unable to move under the belly that choked her face, in the ecstasy of all the flesh that surrounded her from all parts.

The world was finishing in them, as humanity came out of them.

— One could live so until Eternity, said she!

Miss Gregor let go the embrace of her thighs, the pression of her belly came now over her eyes and Reine found herself under her cunt, and with the light, she could admire the navel and all that was above.

— Are you well, darling? questioned the voice of miss Gregor.

— Oh yes, another few minutes of this contemplation.

One would have thought that Reine's body was just born from the womb of the teacher, and that alone the head had to come out from her bowels. The drops of blood on the bottom, which were tending towards the girl's neck gave to such a spectacle a strange and fantastic look.

Reine now turned and kissed at full mouth all the places where there was blood, while miss Gregor wiped them with a handkerchief, so as not to spoil the sheets.

Then, they both jumped down the bed and rapidly, miss Gregor took all her clothes off, made her toilette all naked, and lay down again, the legs well opened, murmuring:

— Kiss me again there a little while, before I give you the whip!

Reine did not want the invitation twice she threw herself on the cunt and clitoris, and ate them with clever and numerous caresses. How she did like such organs: her tongue did not stop, going all through the vagina, where she sometimes tried to put the nose in. Miss Gregor was maddening with that child's game, and she was not long coming.

— Pass me the whip, and I'll whip you quietly first, to let you know the pleasure it gives, said the teacher.

Whip in hand she told Reine to lay flat on her own body so that both their clitoris would touch one another. She beat her slightly at first, then harder, and each blow the girl's body was shivering, so that at each movement, both clitoris were hurting one another frequently. Volupty was such in both that they called attention not to separate and to keep their position up.

Reine did not feel the whip: she did not suffer but, on the contrary felt a want of lust, greater still. The clitoris did not stop rubbing now, and both, woman and child, were under the impression of an intense joy. The whip was thrown aside and, brutally, miss Gregor put her index up Reine's bottom-hole, who almost howled, but she was stopped by a kiss on her lips.

This was followed by an orgy of sucking and fingering, on both parts. The defied each other who should go further, using all the fingers.

There was no more distance of age or social situation: they were getting excited and did not fatigue going from cunt to bottom-hole.

The game pleased them, they were in turn, rolling over and under, so that the one who was sodding the other with the finger pressed also her cheeks between the first one's thighs.

At last they rolled into 69, and really thought they should not be able to separate.

At that time, Mary was not of Reine's thoughts entirely, and when, half dead, she left miss Gregor to go back to her room, she inquired:

— Shall I ever kiss you again?

— Don't doubt it, darling!

CHAPTER V

Happily, miss Gregor had full authority on what was left of girls and servants in the school, for the next day Reine could hardly stand up, having hardly any idea either about the teacher or Mary.

She was allowed to go to bed all the afternoon, and to bed at once again immediately after meals. Miss Gregor, afraid of consequences, intended putting a stop to her own lust, and to let Reine amuse herself with Mary, so as to keep out of touch her own responsibility, in case of accident.

But next morning, Reine was all right again. And she was then pleased to see Mary come back to her and say:

— What was the matter with you, Reine? Were you ill?

— I was sorry, for you evaded me, Mary, the day before yesterday, when you knew well how I desired you.

— Oh, I was not well, meself. I won't have that any more, for we would become ill and fall in some catastrophe for certain.

— No more?

Reine was so sad, that Mary continued:

— I don't want to get you into trouble. If you think it over, you'll see yourself that it is much better we should only chat, as now, instead of giving way to shameful practice.

— That's not what you thought at the infirmary. Someone has talked you over.

— No, Reine, don't believe it. I have a great affection and sympathy for you. If you only contented kissing my face, I would not mind giving you rendez-vous, but all the rest is dirt!

— Who said that?

— Nobody, for you may be sure I did not take anybody in my confidence, to receive any advice.

— Well, after what happened between us,

I cannot renounce to a pleasure I saw you taste! Never mind if it was dirty, I would do any thing dirty with you, and I beg of you, if you love me a trifle, go and wait for me in the music room, where I'll give you a warm caress.

— No, not again, or at least not like the other night in the infirmary. If you must caress me under my dress, let it be at a place where I know I shan't wet.

— Where's that?

— On my bottom and not in front.

— As you like. Your bottom is very nice and it will help me to tame you.

— Is it true that French women like to lick other people's bottoms?

— Story! Certainly you must have spoken to someone. French or English women, we are all the same. When we love, we love all that is the beloved being! I love you, but not you me, or you would understand that kind of caress.

— Oh, yes, dear Reine, I do love you, don't cry. I'll go to the music-room at once but don't let us stay there long.

After all, Reine felt happy, and a few minutes afterwards both friends were together in the room. Mary was already in hiding behind the piano, waiting for Reine.

She kneeled down at once to glide under her dress.

Mary turned her back at once, and pulled up her dress at once:

— Oh, Reine, you go there at once before kissing me on the face! There only, you know!

Reine was already kissing the two twin cheeks through the open drawers, and then a bit of tongue in the slit. Mary murmured:

— You trouble me, make your tongue go well, I like that.

— I'll send you mad.

And Reine was giving great licks, while Mary opened herself with both hands her drawers as much as she could.

At that moment, the door opened and closed. Mary let her dress fall down at once, while Reine hid behind a curtain. Who was there? Miss Gregor? She was not afraid of her. A voice said:

— Allo, here, Mary?

— Yes, I was looking at that music-book.

— So? I thought I saw the French girl come in here too!

— It is an error, Anna.

Anna was a class companion of Mary. Reine understood it all at once. Mary had taken that girl in her confidence, who for some reason or other declared herself the adversary of their passion. She did not admit that moral or chastity could have brought such a change. Anna started again:

— You told me what sympathy you felt for the foreigner, and that it turned to love. I put you on your guard. French women are piggish. If such love amuses you, make her lick your bottom, nothing else. And then, where you'll understand what trifle it all is, you'll listen to me, Mary, and will give me these caresses, I desire so much to know.

— Silly. Never shall I kiss you so!

— Oh, you selfish girl! You let her lick your bottom, but won't lick mine, when I should so much like to see your face here underneath you know what I promised you. Your people are not very rich, and mine are immensely. You have dear tastes and out of school you'll have difficulties. My purse is always full, I put it at your disposal. Let me be your discreet confident, and I'll help you with all I can. Mary, don't be silly, let us come to an understanding before we leave for Scotland, and that won't be long now.

I'm sure if I asked the French girl, I should not have to beg long. I'll prove you so, that with such people, women don't think of love in these caresses, but only about dirtiness.

— Anna, leave me. I'm here to look for a piece of music in that book, and you hinder me.

— Look at my purse, Mary, there are 12 pounds in it with which you could do many things.

— How curious you are with your offers of money!

— Will you have it?

— Leave me alone, go or I'll be cross.

— Take the purse in your hand, there's no harm.

See how the coins are bright and new.

Reine, boiling with rage, heard the nervous laugh of Mary and the sound of gold.

— You'll come to it, said Anna, keep them.

— No, take them away.

— Don't say you wish to give them back

to me. And, after all, it's very little. I'm as king to you, you know such caresses, it won't be much trouble for you to give them to me. You'll give me back that money to-morrow. I tell you, if you won't accept, I shall go to your French girl, and take her away from you.

— I don't think so.

— I understand. Perhaps she's hiding here?

— No Anna, I assure you.

— I am willing to believe you, but keep the purse. We'll talk the matter over again and if your French girl won't take any body in your place, if you are stubborn, I'll denounce you to miss Sticker.

— You would do it?

At that moment we all heard miss Gregor's voice.

— Well, miss, and what are you doing here? No music playing but a tête à tête!

— Don't scold me, miss. Mary was study-ing a piece of music and I only asked her some information. I'll leave her at once.

— All right, come on, said miss Gregor, taking her with her and closing the door.

Mary and Reine were alone once more.

The last named came out of hiding, pale with rage. She caught Mary looking at the gold.

— Oh, Mary, so you took that beast of a girl in your confidence? I feel it, you'll give way.

— No never, Reine.

But she put the purse in her pocket and followed Reine behind the piano.

— I'd love you to kiss me, but I shall never kiss. Let us begin again. Miss Gregor is gone with Anna.

— I won't kiss you, said Reine. You'll be my beloved and you'll remain it. I love you. And as I won't have you say that French girls are piggish, as I am the lover, you'll kiss me.

— I? I told you just now I should never do it!

— If you love me, you'll prove it, by doing it without me paying your caresses with gold.

— My dear, you would not have to give me any money, and perhaps for you should the word: never! not exist, but I'm afraid my caresses would excite you, make you ill...

— You would stop at that?

— Yes. Anna is a bad girl who wanted us to be bad friends, she told me girls killed themselves caressing too much for love. The other day she told me, if you kissed me in front, I should become consumptive. She thought we would become too friendly. The pig! I love you too and I understand your desire for my kisses. Yes, I'll lick you too, as you did me and if French girls are piggish, English ones have nothing to envy them about that.

— Mary, my Mary!

— Show it quick, I'm sure it is nicer than mine.

— Oh no!

— Oh yes!

Mary was down and pulling Reine's dress up.

— You have no drawers?

— I did not notice it.

— Is that the way to pass the tongue?

— Mary, let me lick you!

— Wait, let me prove you I love you.

The English girl got excited, making "feuilles de rose" and "minette" altogether, tossing her off. But the music room was not the place for a long tête à tête, and Reine begged her to stop.

She consented at last and said:

— Yes, we must part. We should do too big things. We'll meet again and will love each other. Look out for opportunities, I'll do the same. Go now. Come and meet me on the terrace or in the park. It is not forbidden during the holidays.

Reine left Mary. On the landing, on the first step she saw miss Gregor who made a sign for her to follow her.

She obeyed and when in the teacher's room, miss Gregor threw herself on the bed, pulled up her dress high up and showing her cunt, said to Reine:

— I favoured your meetings with Mary, now quick, come and "gougnotte" me, make me come to reward me.

Reine saw the splendid thighs and belly which she loved so: she threw herself on it avidly and her little tongue worked so quick, that soon miss Gregor danced up on the back, holding her mouth hard on the clitoris and vagina.

— You are lovely, my little "gougnotte", do it again, it's running, swallow it all, and go away, you would kill me.

Reine wanted no telling, her tongue was going through all traces of wet! Then, passing her arm under miss Gregor's back, she touched the bottom-hole and asked:

— Will you here too?

The teacher kissed her on the lips, and answered:

— No, not yet, darling, we must take advantage of the three or four days we have before leaving for Scotland. There, other cares will separate us, and I shall not be so free as here.

Here, I have full powers, do what you like, as long as you do not become ill. But, be careful about Anna!

Reine's head was turning, when she left the teacher, and she was wondering whom she liked best, Mary or miss Gregor. The first one spoke rather to her heart. She joined her on the park, where, sitting on a bench she was reading, with Anna by her side.

She approached and as miss Gregor had told her to do what pleased her — said boldly:

— Miss Mary, come with me a moment on the terrace, I've something to tell you.

Both Anna and Mary looked at her in

surprise! What! Reine did not care about the rules of the school, forbidding relationships between pupils? Anna turned up her nose, Mary smiled and got up:

— With pleasure, Reine.

— Should I be too much in the conversation, inquired Anna?

— Yes, answered Reine dryly.

— You'll be sorry for it, cried Anna.

— We'll see!

Full with rage, Anna sat down, while both the other girls went.

— You are wrong to talk so harsh to her! She has no other friend but me and is not so bad.

— You gave her back the purse?

Mary blushed.

— I did not think of it.

— I you like, I'll give it back?

— Silly! She would think at once we agree about our little piggish ways, and I swore we both wouldn't do it any more, so that she should not denounce us.

— You were right, but give her back the purse.

— Sure. Why did you call me?

— For a chat. I spoke to miss Gregor

about some good advice you gave me in the infirmary about my studies, and she allowed me to be your companion, all the days we should remain here.

— What strange a permission!

But Mary, too busy about another matter, did not question any more. She liked to be with the French girl who told her her passion very warmly. They walked together, and not a moment did they think of erotism. They chatted for more than an hour, and arranged a meeting for that night.

It was no use thinking about the infirmary now, and boldly Reine said she would join Mary in her bed-room. Mary protested against such temerity. This exasperated her little friend who threatened to whip her, if she did not receive her well in her bed-room, and to make a scandal.

Mary had a special reason to try and dissuade Reine, for she had accepted Anna's purse, promising to join her in her room and execute the caresses so bought.

CHAPTER VI

That night, miss Sticker's severe establishment witnessed a series of adventures which
one finds only in very free schools, such as
Mrs Julie Pouvery's.

As six young ladies were only there, Mary
and Anna, the two big ones, retired quietly,
without being accompanied, and the four
little ones went to bed under the surveyance
of miss Gregor.

Anna winked at Mary, who made an
affirmative sign of the head, and both
entered quickly in Anna's room.

— At last, said Anna, you are reasonable.

— Don't let us be long, Anna, I am

afraid.

— Silly! Miss Gregor is surveying the little ones.

— Never mind, we don't know what might happen.

— You are more, plucky, with that dirty French girl!

Mary blushed, but did not answer. She noticed that her stupidity had put her now at the mercy of her companion.

Anna was taking her things off, and was looking maliciously and spitefully.

— Mary, don't you think surprising the liberty she had all day long?

— Never mind that French girl!

— Yes, let us think of ourselves, but I want to savour before hand, in thought, the sweet relations we are going to have together. There, now I am in my chemise, and we can begin with a first series of caresses.

— A first series?

— Yes! I hope you'll serve me at my fancy, because I love you and will prove it. There was 12 pounds in my purse, it is not enough, here is another 8 pounds. With that amount, you'll give me all your love and will do anything.

— Eight pounds! Oh, Anna, how nice of you! Quick, give me your bottom, I'll eat it up with caresses and licks.

Anna pulled up her chemise, and showed her pointed bottom-cheeks, resembling pears. They looked more like those of a boy than a girl's, but did not displease Mary who, having put the 8 pounds in her pocket, licked the bottom conscientiously.

— How nice, cried Anna, your tongue is. Go further inside, Mary, it's burning! Wait, I'll lie on the bed, it will be easier for you.

Mary was decided to satisfy Anna in all she wanted. A companion who makes a present of 20 pounds, is well worth some pleasure to give. And such caresses tickle the flesh, and prepare the understanding of the beauty of piggish acts.

Anna was certainly not a handsome girl; no, she was even ugly, but her eyes were alight with diabolical looks and she had a pussy very black and thick hanging low down on the thighs.

Well placed on the bed, the bottom high up she called to Mary:

— There, push the tongue right in.

Mary bent down, and shameless pointed her tongue right on the centre of the slit, working with little blows, so as Reine had done with her.

Under such work, Anna moved about, got on her knees, opened the thighs, put the head of her companion underneath, saying:

— This is the prolongation of the bottom, send your little tongue that way.

Mary licked the cout, sucked the clitoris, and started again the "feuilles de rose". Anna was moving about more and more, laughing tickled, but did not come.

All at once she laid down on the belly, sighed and cried!

— Oh Mary! you produce such effect on me, I am ill! One moment, stop, or I'm not sure of anything!

Surprised, Mary stopped, and inquired:

— What's the matter? Have you enough of it and shall I go?

— No, no, I have not vibrated yet! Oh! oh! Mary excuse me, but wait here for me, I must leave the room a while. Don't attempt to go, or I'll pursue you right in your room, and I won't be spiteful.

— Where are you going?

— To the... I have some belly-ache.

— Oh!

Mary made a grimace, where she saw her friend run away, after she had put a petticoat on. She tried to go, but Anna turned round, and speaking hard and drily, she whispered:

— Stop, you hear, or you'll regret it!

Decidedly the poor little fair one was afraid of her companion: her heart was beating hard, thinking of the danger she was exposed to and of Anna's future exigencies. Then she was disgusted, but did not have the necessary energy to fly away. She was still there, when Anna reappeared, the face full of satisfaction.

— Right, said she, you are waiting for your little food! You'll have it, for I'm better now! Go, go, Mary, your tongue will only procure me pleasure now.

— What, Anna, you?...

— Go on, I say. It'll go all by itself! She laid on the bed again. Mary closed the eyes. Was Anna joking? What, not a drop of water to wash it? Anna grew impatient, pulled up her bottom and ordered:

— Your tongue at once, lazy girl! Do you

think I am dirty, and that I did not use any paper? Start immediately, I desire to be licked so!

Mary got up resolutely and answered:

— I will not lick you, if you do not wash!

— You won't lick me! Very well, give me my purse back and my money. No, I'll go down and call miss Gregor, and I'll tell her you have robbed me, also that I found you in my room when I came back from the w. c.

— Anna! do be quiet!

— Lick me.

— Yes, yes.

— Very well!

Mary begun again on the bottom of Anna: first she worked quietly, then with a mad ardour, hoping to hasten the pleasure. Suddenly they heard a voice through the keyhole:

— You pigs, patience! Miss Gregor will pay you!

With one jump, Mary got up, Anna did the same and pushed her towards the door:

— I'm sure it's that French girl spying us. I'll pay her. Run away.

Mary trembled as a leaf; but she had only to fly. Opening the door quietly and noticing nobody in the corridor, she ran to her room and entered quickly, when she saw Reine before her, watching her disdainfully:

— You, you with that dirty girl, and so ugly too! I would not go to miss Gregor, because I love you so; but it's all over between us!

Mary kneeled down, kissed Reine's dress, murmuring:

— Reine, you don't know!...

— Yes, I know. It is for money you licked that bottom... full of caca!...

— No, no, there was none!...

— She would not wash herself, I heard her. Let me alone, I forbid you to kiss me. Leave me! I will not have any more to do with you. I had come in your room, thinking you would be back, and hoping to convince you to keep me, even willing to force you to it. And you see, I brought the whip with me.

I loved you, as I esteemed you were as pure as lovely! You see, I did not go to call miss Gregor, as I threatened you both with, but came instead to your room to tell you to go to bed quietly. The teacher will not know anything, but remember, I forbid you in future, to speak to me, on the terrace or any where else.

— Hit me, whip me, Reine darling, but love me still!

— Good-by miss Mary, I won't prevent you picking up miss Anna's gold.

Mary took her by the legs, she admired really that child who was pushing her back to her dirt.

She kissed her dress, hands, tried to pull up her petticoats. Reine struggled, got wild, and at last hit her with the handle of the whip on the fingers, struck her in the face, and Mary left her alone, irritated with her resistance and with the blows.

— You'll be sorry for it, Reine, she said simply.

— Good-by, miss Mary, you exist no more for me.

— We'll see about that!

Reine left her: she went back to her room, through the corridors, lit only by the beams of the moon coming through the high windows. She fancied she heard a noise and was frightened. The great house full of silence and without lights acted on her mind. She was not mistaken. Someone was walking in the gallery, near-bye: it was the heavy foot-step of a man.

Astonished, she ran and hid in the folds of a big curtain, keeping her breath up. A man was passing-by she could not recognise, but who seemed to try to find his way, uncertain, for he was stopping at times. Was it a burglar? Feebly he called:

— Margaret?

She was reassured now. Margaret was the servant left to miss Gregor. The man knew her then, as he was going about on the floor right beneath the one where was Margaret's room.

He was feeling his way now, from door to door, but none opened. Moved by curiosity, she followed him silently in the dark, but stopped stupefied: he had pushed the door of Mary's room and had gone in. What did it all mean? She trembled with fear and now heard her friend cry one loud cry, as if in pain. Reine was as if in a vertigo, and she fell down in a heap.

What would it have been, had she witnessed the tragedy that was being enacted in the room she had just left a moment before? The man had entered the room. Mary was astonished to find him there instead of Reine, thinking it was the French girl who had altered her mind and come back. The man too was thunder struck. But Mary's fright and emotion rendered her so beautiful, that as a brute, the man who was a gardener, Margaret's lover, did not hesitate: he jumped on her, threw her on the bed and attacked her with fury.

She struggled instructively first, then wished to call, but the man's hand closed her mouth and prevented her. He was very strong, and knew what he wanted, so that nothing could have saved Mary from such embrace.

He kept her between his legs firmly, undid his tie and used it for her as a gag, and mastered her with such vigour, that she had to open her legs and give way.

A deep trouble paralysed her: she kept conscious and breathed hard through the folds of the tie. He had threatened to strangle her if she made the least noise. Her thighs aspired the prick that split them, she was not coming and felt no pleasure but no pain, obeying to the impulse that had put her in the proper position to lose her maidenhead.

Her only thought was not to be strangled or murdered. Never mind her virtue, her chastity, her pudor. Half the work was over now, her fragile virginity did not exist any longer, and the prick was conquering the vagina, making her bleed. The outrage she was submitted to, her sufferings gave a little more energy to her will; and such will turned to the ease of the coït which she favoured still by her soft attitude. Then the man said:

— If you keep quiet, and don't cry, I'll take away the tie.

She pulled her head down, as a consent, and the tie was taken away from her mouth. She let him do it, stupidly passive, bit her lips to stop any complaint, while he pursued the volupty by taking her maidenhead. She felt robust hands pulling her flesh about, and smelt the strong odour of the male. Had she not licked Anna's bottom, coming from the w. c.? Nothing was to disgust her now. She gave way to the desire that outraged her, she neared her belly, gave herself away and when the sperm came, she jumped as much by satisfied lust as by terror.

A man possessed her in this house where

no man was allowed. He had come, and was dressing himself up again.

While she was still on the bed, he got a big knife out of his pocket, showed it to her and told her not to say a word, or he would cut her throat.

She trembled and he went away quietly. A terrible anguish took her then: her garments spoiled, the sheets, all the trouble around every thing would tell, she was done for, and not only that, but the man would kill her besides. Quick! although full of emotion and tired out in all her limbs, she must save all appearances! She was virgin no more! What would result of it all? Why did Reine leave her? Nothing would have happened!

With haste, she repaired all damage, and fortunately she had come queer during the work, bloodstains would not surprise, and then, damning what was done now, she went to bed, wept and slept.

CHAPTER VII

When Reine came to her senses again every thing was in silence around her: had she been the joke of a dream? One moment she thought it. She got up on her knees and crawled to Mary's room, looked through the keyhole and saw her in bed asleep.

Afraid again she ran to her own room, in another part of the building, and went to bed also.

The next day, nobody would have thought what happened in the night, and life began like before. Mary only was very pale, and looked disdainfully at Reine, while she went herself to Anna with whom she remained.

Reine felt a great trouble at heart: fancy a man is miss Sticker's school! She could say nothing of what she had seen in the gallery. She feared mockery and sarcasms, and how to explain her presence.

To go to miss Gregor — also she herself feared nothing — was it not to denounce Mary and Anna, and bring punishment to them? *By whip and by rod!* How to know about that man?

She made up her mind to stop Mary and ask her for an explanation. She saw her alone and approached her:

— Miss Mary did you sleep well last night?

— I forbid you to speak to me!

— I regret that you should answer me in such manner; because I shall ask miss Gregor for such explanation.

— Go, you tell-tale, nothing surprises me from you.

— I am no tell-tale, miss Mary, but after I left you, I had some hallucination, I suppose, it seemed to me someone was entering your room; I was going to your help, when I fell in a dead faint.

Mary frowned:

— You are mad, as every one in your country! Go and tell your stories to miss Gregor.

Anna joined Mary who said to her:

— Anna shall we go to the music-room?

— Miss Mary, interrupted Reine, I shall not importune you any longer, but I won't hear any thing bad said about my country and you'll be sorry for what you have said just now, as you promised me I should be sorry because I would not associate with your dirty ways.

— Shall I slap your face, asked Anna, you impertinent hussy?

— Try, was Reine's answer, and you'll know about it. Go to the music-room: if you come out of the w. c., miss Mary will lick your bottom and save you paper!

Mad with rage the two English girls were ready to jump on her, when miss Gregor appeared, calling:

— Miss Reine, I was looking for you. Come on.

She glanced defiantly at Mary and Anna, and ran to the teacher.

— Come to my room to repeat the lesson.

Her heart was now beating with pleasure: the teacher liked her, she was under her protection. Silently she followed her, and as soon as in her room, she fell in her arms and kissed her with fury, while the teacher was surprised of such tender feelings, in companion with the pleasure she intended having.

— What is the matter, my little "gougnotte", you kissing me in such a manner? Have you anything particular to ask me for? Speak out. Kiss me there quick.

— Oh yes, for ever, dear teacher, but I should like to speak to you before.

— Speak quick. Look at that little bud that wants your tongue!

— I'll eat it up, don't be afraid. All day and all night, if you like.

— Are you cross with Mary then? I heard you when you left her room, and did not come out of mine.

— Yes, we are on bad terms! Listen, I did not want to denounce her, but she acts too badly! Yes I went to see her, but she was in Anna's room!

— Miss Anna's room? Surely?

— I heard their conversation and I looked.

Miss Anna gave her some money to lick her bottom; then she ran to the w. c. because she had the belly-ache, and when returning obliged Mary to kiss it again. It disgusted me indeed.

— I am so surprised that it takes away from me all desire of being kissed there. This is very serious. I'll see you to-night instead of now, and that will make us ever so much more gluttonous. How could Mary have accepted money from Anna, and how could this one have such a fancy? Do they think you'll denounce them?

— Perhaps! I threatened them, because they spoke spitefully to me.

— Well, they must not believe that you have denounced them; I'll manage to take them by surprise somehow either here or in Scotland. Did you quarrel with miss Mary?

— I waited for her in her room and told what I thought of her.

— Why did you not come to me at first?

— I did not wish to denounce her. And then another thing happened, and here I do not know if I dreamt or not! I saw a man entering miss Mary's room and I her heard her utter a cry.

Miss Gregor's pallor troubled Reine, who said:

— Perhaps I have dreamt. I fell on the floor, unconscious, and when I came to my senses, I went to Mary's room and saw her asleep.

— You must have made a mistake! Never mind this is much more serious, and I must survey all this affair carefully. In both our interests, it is necessary that you should get friendly again with this Mary I have always detested, and now more than ever. There is great danger in your quarrel. Miss Sticker will not let any one go against the rules.

— Get friendly with Mary?

— You loved her yesterday. Forget what took place.

— I'll try, miss Gregor, to show you how much I love you.

— Thank you, darling, go back to the three little girls, and choose your time to approach miss Mary.

But such time did not come, for Anna never left Mary; both had perhaps suspicions about the teacher's relationship with Reine, anyhow they surveyed miss Gregor, who knowing she was guilty, did not wish to go in a temper and dare not call Reine to her room.

This went on until the departure for Scotland, where they arrived safely.

Although not so severe as at school, miss Sticker was still terrifying. She lived in a big estate, amidst some members of her family, two teachers and miss Gregor specially affected to the conduct of the pupils. These could run about, take all sorts of recreations, but were not allowed to speak at table. After supper there was some music and even dancing going on, miss Sticker's young nephews teaching waltz and lancers to the girls.

Life was not at all unpleasant there.

Miss Gregor seemed to forget the trouble brought on by Reine's confession to her, and did not think of any relationship with her, leaving her with the youngest pupils, three young girls of the 2nd division, allowing reading or solitary walks. Anna and Mary were still hostile to her.

Three parts of the holidays had passed over quietly, when, one evening, as Reine had had a dance with a teacher, she overheard Anna saying to Mary:

— The Frenchy will tell-tale and make us punished after the vacation.

She pretended not to have heard, but following her closely, she met her alone in an alley of the garden, and losing no time in unnecessary threats, jumped on her and slapped her face.

— You pig, cried Anna, I'll pay you for your treachery.

— Shitty bottom, answered Reine, give one of my slaps to Mary from me.

Anna was blind with passion; taking Reine with a grip, they both struggled and the blows with fists and feet were coming down hard. They rolled down, and the noise of the struggle was at last heard by a servant, who ran to them, separated the girls and brought them back to the house.

Miss Sticker's stupefaction was extreme. She called at once the two teachers and miss Gregor. As a rule there was no punishment during the vacation, but here the case was so serious that a rigorous punishment imposed itself.

Miss Sticker did not suspect the cause of such animosity between pupils of two different divisions.

Certainly Reine was precocious in her intellectual and physical development, but she was still with the young girls, while Anna was with the big ones. What could have caused a quarrel? Nobody knew anything about it, and the two culprits kept silent before the questions.

Miss Gregor questioned also, said bravely she had not noticed anything.

Miss Sticker ordered the punishment of the rod for the two fighters, punishment to be applied at once by miss Gregor.

— One will begin with you, miss Anna; I advise you to be quiet, otherwise it will be done before all girls assembled, and entirely naked. Now, come, and take your drawers off and pull up your dress. Anna knew there was no resistance to be made. She obeyed, let the garments fall down and exhibited her thin bottom pear shaped, with thin legs; she trembled, and shut her eyes, when she saw miss Gregor coming with a small stick in hand, instead of the rod that could not be found anywhere.

The stick whistled, cut the flesh, and Anna howled desperately; the cheeks so thin and the little muscles vibrated with more force; so the suffering was acuter. She tried to put her hands to save her bottom; bad idea, for the stick came down a second time, but on the fingers, and Anna, mad with pain and rage, ran for the door.

But at the door there were servants in waiting.

— Miss Anna, said miss Sticker's cold voice, come back at once, and pull up your skirt, so as to finish the correction you have deserved through your fault. You expose yourself to get the part of punishment I reserved to miss Reine.

— That dirty French girl! cried Anna. Who slapped me without provocation and with whom I fought only to protect meself.

— At last, you say something about the quarrel! Is it true, miss Reine?

— It was under provocation. She had accused me to spy to tell-tale to the teachers, when returning to school.

— When did she say that?

— Yesterday. After the dance.

— And you waited till to-day to slap her face! This is more serious because it shows revenge and premeditation, that must be corrected. I won't come back over my sentence, but you are the biggest culprit of the two. Pull up your dress, miss Anna.

— What, after her confession, you pretend to punish me still?

— No discussion, please. As she won't obey, undress her naked, and I'll call here the whole household to witness it all.

— Oh no! I'll obey, but miss Gregor beats too hard.

Not to hit so hard? Miss Gregor had taken some of Reine's dislike, for that girl nagged her. She sent a blow that marked a line, white at first, then red across the cheeks.

— I'm dying, she murders me, vociferated Anna, rolling over the carpet.

Two more blows sent her in convulsions, the servants came at once, held her by the arms and pulling her skirts right up the back.

— Mercy! pity!

— We are not so severe here as at school, said miss Sticker, we'll stop your punishment, miss Anna, and we might have stopped before, if you had not showed such resistance. Your turn now, miss Reine, take your drawers off and pull up your skirts.

Some months before, the French girl

would have revolted more than Anna; but miss Gregor awaited and looked on: she knew that she would hit with less cruelty, on account of their mutual erotic affection; and if the blows were hard and sounded, they would be applied so as not to make her body and moral suffer. So taking no notice of the feminine looks converging upon her, she undid her drawers, took them off, pulled up her skirts and showed her plump bottom before miss Gregor's eyes.

It was not thin and poor as Anna's; the two round cheeks announced the ripening fruit, and if not as ample as those of a woman, they showed as much perfection in the harmony of shapes and flesh.

Tender girl's bottom, well designed, with apples full and calling the kiss. It was not afraid of the threatening flagellation, but seeming to bow gracefully before the looks which were in contemplation, looks of women, teachers and servants, devoid of severity.

Miss Sticker's eyes even fixed on those of miss Gregor, indicating she would be approved in her leniency, Anna was in rage with this leniency, that she could notice from the place where she stood, crying on the sofa.

Miss Gregor was going to pull up the arm to hit, but the hand came down and caressed the cheeks lightly with the stick. The blows were going crescendo: Reine was full of gratefulness but bent her head down, not to show all the love she had for the teacher.

No one disapproved of miss Gregor for the way she proceeded: the French girl's bottom was cracking under the blows, reddening with purple marks. She did not sigh, did not cry, and miss Gregor could hold the arm right up, make the stick whistle, hit, the mad crisis of Anna's pain was over, and did not begin again.

— That will do, miss Gregor, said miss Sticker, this child supported with courage her torture, much harder than that of miss Anna. Bring her to her room, and heal her, for fear she would suffer.

— She was whipped not so hard as I was, cried Anna!

— Just the same, and longer! If you protest, we'll start again!

Anna did not wish it; a servant brought her to her room, to apply some calming ointment on her scratched bottom.

Reine, alone with miss Gregor, went on her knees, murmuring:

— Thank you miss, with all my heart, you have spared me and I love you. Say, let me "gougnotte" you like over there, but alas, I am no more your "gougnotte"!

— Circumstances are not favourable, dear! No, I have not spared you. I am using you to flagellation, that is a source of pleasure for one who knows how to appreciate it and get over the pain. Have you suffered much?

— Not as much as I feared.

— Show me your little bottom.

— Show me yours, miss, and mine will be healed.

— Little devil, you are then always thinking about such things? Give me your bottom, I'll put some ointment on it; I'll give you mine for a few seconds.

Reine was nursed by miss Gregor but declared she did not suffer, so as to satisfy quicker the desire that began to upset her again; and when at last the teacher pulled up her own skirts, she threw herself on her bottom as a bitch, and kissed them so that the other one sighed.

— You little devil! You are born for it, there, I give way, "gougnotte" me, make me come and I'll run away.

She crossed over her head to show her the thighs well open, put her clitoris on her lips and the kissing resulted soon: the coming was wetting the vagina, the teacher held Reine's face to her cunt, and she aspired with lust the dew of love.

CHAPTER VIII

From that day, Anna's hate followed Reine step by step, for she wished to take her revenge for the slaps in the face and the physical correction. Having more and more power over Mary, she made her have the same manner of thinking and both were studying the ways to torture the French girl.

Sexual relations between the two had changed: Anna's authority had turned towards Mary's soft nature to make of her passive of lesbian acts begun before the departure for Scotland.

After a few times, as she could not satisfy her lust with "feuilles de rose", she obliged

Mary to do her, she looked at her with more attention, notice her lovely face, as Reine had done, threw her on her back behind a bush, and kissed her with such ardour that she made her come.

— What, said Mary? you kiss and lick now!

— For ever will I kiss and lick you! I feel it more so. Let me suck your bottom-hole now.

— Not here, but come in the loft right at the top of the house, where we are allowed to take a view of the scenery.

They were not watched here in Scotland as at school, we have said it. The house had lofts to warehouse vegetables, fruits, which were afterwards sent to London. In the middle was a belvedere with a balcony wherefrom there was a splendid view. It was thus easy for the girls to go up and hide in the lofts. Miss Sticker suspected nothing, as she did not suppose of evil; it was Reine's arrival that had opened Mary ideas, and Mary had communicated them to Anna. And miss Gregor was no pupil.

The two lovers agreed about the loft and went there by two different ways. They found a small room with two doors that gave all safety to be desired. Some sacks were there and Anna showed one to Mary to lean on.

— Your bottom, quick!

Mary had already the skirts on the shoulders, the bottom out of the drawers, and Anna's tongue worked so masterfully that both came.

Anna felt a strong pleasure and the lesbian bond getting tighter; they achieved debauching one another, vowing an eternal love.

That corner of the loft — they called it their Eden — received their frequent visits. Who would have suspected them? For they knew how to choose the moments their solitude would not be disturbed.

They exchanged ideas, in such unceasing lustful relationship, and Reine was often the subject of the conversations. A same temper against the French girl animated them and searched for a manner to ill treat her.

With diabolical patience they were planning to bring her to some trap, where they would torture her, and pleased at the thought of the punishment they would have to receive for it afterwards.

Mary, taking advantage that Reine looked at her with more sadness than irritation, pretended to be better disposed towards her, and murmured one afternoon to her:

— Shall we then always be bad friends?

— You wish it, Mary.

— I? Don't you remember how spiteful you were for a mere nothing? I loved you, Reine, and if you were disgusted, you only had to let yourself be caressed, as I did it in the afternoon! I should have been your lover, is it not natural? I am the eldest!

— You'll never know, Mary, how I loved you! Oh! for my torture when I saw you in that bitch of Anna's room! You so nice, handsome, ideal in beauty. I could have licked your footsteps, and you go and dirt your mouth on her beastly skin!

— And you love me no more!

The voice was insinuating. Now Mary, débauchée, knew besides how to use her eyes, face, and attitudes. Reine sighed. She wanted the pleasures which had caused her exile from France. She had found her lover again, the sweet one she had deeply loved before the holidays, with whom she had had so many volupties.

After all, why should she not forget? Mary was following the work of thoughts passing through her mind. She took her hand and murmured:

— Reine, darling, I also loved you much! You revealed to me a lust I had ignored. Why should we not still love... a little?

— No, I won't! You are too much Anna's friend to understand the adoration I vowed to you! Don't let us be cross, and we'll forget the past.

— You did not love me, and I have been wrong in stopping you here.

Mary let Reine's hand go and pretended to leave, but Reine stopped her.

— Please, don't think I did not love you.

— If it is so, you should want me still, and you would not dispute me to Anna, who persecutes me with her love and whom I should tell to go.

A trouble was all over Reine. Mary sought her, and she was not running after her volupties. She believed her. She was living her first emotions over again: the night at the infirmary, and the beautiful white and delicate body, animated by her caresses. Her senses woke up again.

— I should love you still, if you were not so independent, Mary.

She shivered, while Mary's eyes showed a look of triumph: she whispered in her ear:

— Come up to the loft. Wait for me by the belvedere, I'll show you a small room where nobody will prevent us to judge if we still love one another.

— No, Mary, I won't.

— I order it. Come up, Reine, I'll do you what you'll do me. We must come together. I want you as you want me.

Reine was intoxicated with the charm of a voice she had not heard for long and that spoke amorously. She did not resist to the temptation and obeyed. Mary followed her with her look, and as soon as she could not be seen, she ran to an alley where she knew she would find Anna.

— Quick, run up to our Eden. Hide behind the sacks, I'll bring Reine, and we'll do what we like with her.

She was pleased with her treachery. They did not exchange a word, knowing they would agree about the evil to do.

Reine was upstairs, full of joy, and hid behind a balcony until Mary came up.

— Are you there, Reine? did she ask quietly, as the place was half in darkness.

— Here, Mary.

— Right.

They were face to face. Mary picked up her dress quickly and showed her naked thighs.

— See, I'm ready, if you will do it.

— Here, no one can surprise us.

— Have you your drawers?

— Yes.

— Take it off. Let us be similar. Leave it behind the pillar, we'll take it afterwards. Mary had progressed since the first times, she stood there, skirts up, tossing off her clitoris.

— Your tongue will produce more effect, but I'm preparing meself.

Reine took her drawers off, and did as Mary told her.

— Show me your belly, if it is as hairy as mine.

— Not here, Mary.

— Lick my bottom before you leave here. I'll judge then, if you still love me. There it is.

Reine did not resist, and sitting on her heels, she threw her tongue in.

— Pig, cried Mary, you do me worse that what I did to Anna. I went to the w. c. an hour ago and did not use any paper. I let it dry. Put your tongue right in the middle, so that I shall forget your insults. Ah, you obey! there, so you love me still? even dirty?

Mad with lust Reine, finding this flesh, she saw them as nice and more knowing, and Mary's observation instead of rebuking her, made her more hardy on the contrary. Yes, she noticed now that she had neglected to ordinary cares, and Reine saw in it the proof that Mary wished to conquer her again.

Her legs were still as nice and white but had a perfume stronger that went to the brain and precipitated the movements of the blood. One must love someone greatly, to show oneself in such manner! At least Reine thought so.

Oh! what a nice odour and how she liked it! And now her whole face was right in the open slit, so much beloved. She licked and licked, saying at last:

— Yes, you are right, I am a pig, but from you every thing should seem good.

A certain emotion went to Mary's heart: at

that moment she understood the diabolical act she was committing and she was ready to tell Reine of it. But she saw Anna who had come up on tip-toes.

— Come, come, Reine, we are not safe here, come further, get up and follow me.

Reine left Mary's cheeks and went to the place they called their Eden.

When getting in, Mary murmured:

— Here we are by ourselves, let us undress: I'll lick you as you did me.

— What you like, Mary.

Mary took her dress off! Reine did the same. There was no danger here in that corner. Mary remained in her petticoat and told her to keep up in her chemise, so as to better caress her, and when she was as she wanted her, she made her lay on a sack so as to better kiss her. Reine prayed her to begin. She answered:

— No, I want to feel the effect of my kisses on your flesh.

Reine managed the best she could on the sack, so that Mary could place her head between her thighs, but before she could move, Anna jumped across her breast, and held her hands in hers: stupor was paralysing Reine, who did not try to defend herself. Mary was tying her legs also. She could not struggle.

Without giving her time or chance to cry, Anna glided from the breast to the head, pulled up her own skirt and placing her cunt, no more veiled than Mary's, over her face, she pissed right on it.

— Take that, waiting for better, she said. Ah! you said Mary was a pig because you surprised her with me. You have nothing to envy her and you are even better served. I piss on your face and we'll see if you dare to go and boast of it to miss Gregor.

— Don't do that, cried Mary.

— It's done, love: unfortunately I did not want it much or she would have had it in the mouth and nose. Now come here and I'll lick you right before her eyes, to teach her I am your lover and not she.

— I won't, replied Mary. Enough of it. What we do is too bad. She had confidence. You are avenged, don't go any further.

— What? we are only beginning and you pretend to renounce to what we have planned? Put yourself well in position above her head, I want her to see me lick you, and my spit will fall on her nose. I'll keep her between my legs, if I come, and that is sure, I'll rub meself on her belly.

— Anna, please.

— Shall I have to beat you too? Here is a whip! I discovered it. Come we'll use it on her bottom. Now then, I'll start with your bottom.

Reine said nothing, what for? She could have made some noise, call attention, and then what could have happened? She might have been thrown out after a sound thrashing. She was at her rival's hands, she must show no failing. Her heart was bleeding at Mary's treachery and she regretted the day she felt on love for her beauty.

Above her head on a pile of sacks Mary was sitting and between her legs, Anna's tongue was working. She had pulled up Reine's chemise and kept her bust between the legs: from time to time the saliva was falling on her face, coming out of Mary's cunt and now, about her navel, she felt Anna's hand tossing herself off.

All at once she saw Mary shivering and coming under the kisses. Anna now also felt

some pleasure and let her cunt fall on her
navel to wipe her own wet.

At that moment the lust was the
strongest. Reine murmured:

— You are silly to tie me up. I should let
you do it.

— Pig, said Anna, I won't have you
coming with what we do.

— Not with what you do, Anna. I detest
you as you detest me. But for Mary and to
prevent her being sorry for her bad action I'll
consent not to move and bear every thing.

— You take me for a fool and think to
make Mary pity you. You are wrong.

She was even more enraged than me
against you and she'll prove it by helping
me to tie you up here, until they come to
look for you, finding you all undressed.
What a scandal! and how I shall laugh at
your punishment. Denounce us, if you dare.

— No, said Mary. Let her be tied until
you are satisfied with your revenge, but I
oppose all consequences with miss Sticker.
Let us make haste, so that we should not be
caught all three.

— Nobody will find us, and I do not
compliment you on the fragility of your

character, Mary. You made her put her drawers on the belvedere so as to well establish her fault, and you go back now. Let her know you combined this little affair. Beautiful French girl, this sweet Mary wanted you to see for yourself how much we love each other. The spectacle we decided to close by taking your dress and drawers and putting it in the drawing room.

Mary renounces to this part of the programme all right. I wanted to whip you with this whip. Show us your bottom, and let it have its ration.

Brutally, she turned Reine over, opened her cheeks, passed her hand over them.

— Your bottom is well made, you'll feel the blows ever so much better. Oh! she is coming. Say, Mary, she wets! That's too much. Well or badly treated, she comes: French girls are all created for dirty things. I'll give you coming!

The whip in hand came down on Reine's bottom: the blow was hard, and a violent shiver moved the girl in her legs and back. She did not cry. Anna was going to start again, but Mary held it up.

— Enough. Do not hit her any more!

— There's for you, answered Anna, getting away and hitting her across the shoulders.

Mary howled under the blow.

Anna threw the whip away and made for the door.

— You fool! run away, your cry must have been heard, and we will be caught.

She came back, for miss Gregor appeared behind her, inquiring:

— What is the matter here? What! a pupil tied up! Why do you cry, miss Mary?

— Anna whipped me because I did not wish Reine to be hit with the whip.

— Miss Reine tied up?

— Mary has her share in it, replied Anna. I took the arms, she took the legs.

— This is very serious.

— Not so much, miss Gregor, said Anna, but it can all be arranged.

— Do you intend dictating me what to do?

Anna looked miss Gregor full in the eyes:

— Ask your bottom licker what has happened and let all the affair go aside, you think we don't take precautions against your indiscretions? Take my advice. Let the affair aside altogether.

— Go to your room, miss Anna, and wait the result of my report to miss Sticker, about what I have seen and the words you have just used.

— Address your report with full details. I shall tell you kept Reine in your room all one night and you surveyed the school so well during miss Sticker's absence that a man entered miss Mary's room and that he outraged her. It is easy to prove. Go and make your report now, miss Gregor.

— Untie the child!

— Right you are. And then let us go with miss Mary, and no more talk about it.

Anna undid Reine of her bounds. Mary dressed her, skirt, drawers and all.

— Can we go, asked Anna mockingly?

— Go, answered simply the teacher.

— Come, Mary, let us leave these two lovers, they'll console one another.

Miss Gregor looked viciously at Anna but said nothing. When they were both gone, she pressed Reine to her heart:

— Darling, we'll revenge ourselves. Mary is as bad as Anna. I'll promise you the most vivid and tender joys during the next schooling. But I must know everything about these two bad girls, so as to have them beaten hard on their bottom so that there won't be a piece of flesh left. Can I rely on you?

— I'll be your "gougnotte".

— Yes, and I'll prevent you from many a trouble.

— They'll pay what they said about you, and their treachery towards me.

— Be artful! and try to reconcile at least with Mary.

— Be sure, I'll be as false as she was and I shall come, the day the whip and the rod will tear up their flesh.

END OF THE FIRST VOLUME

BIRCHGROVE PRESS
Flagellant & Libertine Erotica

—————

Birchgrove Press specializes in producing new print and e-book editions of pre-1950s writings on sexual flagellation in English. Original editions of many of the books that we offer are difficult to obtain and are highly sought after. We are especially proud to offer new editions of rare Victorian flagellant texts such as *The Mysteries of Verbena House*, *Experimental Lecture by Colonel Spanker*, and *The Quintessence of Birch Discipline*. Birchgrove Press also produces new editions of libertine literature. We have published *Venus in the Cloister*, *The School of Venus*, *The Dialogues of Luisa Sigea*, and Isidore Liseux's translation of the Marquis de Sade's *Justine* (1791), *Opus Sadicum*, for example.

www.birchgrovepress.com.

www.ingramcontent.com/pod-product-compliance
Lightning Source LLC
Chambersburg PA
CBHW072004170626
46813CB00005B/2006